For six years of the most terrible war in history, these brave men and women never stopped fighting. They were the underground soldiers. They fought their secret battles in the streets and in prisons and churches. They fought in cities and forests and swamps, from Poland in Eastern Europe to the distant Solomon Islands in the South Pacific.

Their only reward was the knowledge that they had not given up. They had no airplanes, tanks, or artillery. Their weapons were hope and faith and the desire to be free. This is their story.

ARTHUR PRAGER is a free-lance writer whose experience as an Intelligence Officer during World War II has given him special insight into the plight of civilian resisters. His writings include adventure novels for young people. EMILY PRAGER, his daughter, is a free-lance writer whose articles have appeared in many major periodicals. Both live and work in New York City.

LAUREL-LEAF BOOKS bring together under a single imprint outstanding works of fiction and nonfiction particularly suitable for young adult readers, both in and out of the classroom. This series is under the editorship of Charles F. Reasoner, Professor of Elementary Education, New York University.

WORLD WAR II RESISTANCE STORIES

ARTHUR PRAGER AND

EMILY PRAGER

Illustrated by Steven Assel

LAUREL-LEAF BOOKS

Published by
Dell Publishing Co., Inc.
1 Dag Hammarskjold Plaza
New York, New York 10017

Laurel-Leaf Library ® TM 766734, Dell Publishing Co., Inc.

ISBN: 0-440-99800-X

Reprinted by arrangement with Franklin Watts, Inc.

Printed in the United States of America

First Laurel-Leaf printing—August 1980

Contents

Introduction

When an enemy invades a country and takes control of its people, this act is called an "occupation." So far the United States has never been "occupied." Americans have never had to suffer the rule of a foreign and hostile government. And compared to most countries in the world, this makes us very fortunate indeed. England has faced serious danger on several occasions. Napoleon and later Adolf Hitler planned to invade England. Both were defeated by British forces before they could carry out their plans.

Try to imagine what life would be like if an enemy did take control of us. We cannot know for sure what would happen. But it is likely that our rights as citizens would be gone. We would have to obey any laws the enemy might make.

Our military services would be disbanded. Our soldiers, sailors, and marines would have to fight for the enemy or be imprisoned or killed. Those who resisted, or who were suspected of resisting, would be sent to prison camps. If the enemy didn't like a citizen's religion or politics, he or she could be killed without trial.

And, most importantly, we would no longer be free. We would be afraid to walk in our own streets, or to speak openly about our thoughts and ideas.

How would you feel if we were occupied? What would you do? The idea of an occupation probably seems strange and frightening.

This book is about people who lived in occupied countries during World War II. It is the story of men and women who risked their lives to fight the terror and brutality of their invaders. They set up secret resistance groups and saved the lives of thousands of their nations' people.

For six years of the most terrible war in history, these brave men and women never stopped fighting. They were the underground soldiers. They fought their secret battles in the streets and in prisons and churches. They fought in cities and forests and swamps, from Poland in Eastern Europe to the distant Solomon Islands in the South Pacific.

Their only reward was the knowledge that they had not given up. They had no airplanes, tanks, or artillery. Their weapons were hope and faith and the desire to be free. This is their story.

[3]

Chapter I

WITOLD PILECKI

The Nazis invaded Poland in 1939. The German High Command ordered all Polish military officers to surrender and enter prisoner-of-war camps. Those who failed to do so would be sentenced to death. Of the 20,000 officers, only about 400 followed the German order. Most of them joined the Home Army, an underground organization dedicated to resisting the Nazis and helping to free Poland. One of these brave men was an ex-cavalry officer named Witold Pilecki.

A year after the occupation, Pilecki made a plan to help his people. The Germans had built a prison camp near the town of Auschwitz in southern Poland. Thousands of political prisoners were sent there. Among the inmates were many loyal Poles, but they were not organized. They had no leaders. Pilecki decided to go to Auschwitz. He wanted to organize the prisoners so that they could resist the hardships of prison life, help the sick and wounded, and send information back to Home Army headquarters in Warsaw.

The problem Pilecki faced was how to get

into the camp without the Nazi secret police, the dreaded Gestapo, finding out. He came up with a daring plan. There was only one sure way. He would allow himself to be arrested!

One morning Pilecki left his home and began to walk toward the middle of Warsaw. He carried a forged identity card. If all went well, the Gestapo would never find out his real name or suspect that he was on a secret mission. If they discovered his true identity, he would certainly be shot.

Trucks rattled by as he walked. Country folk passed him, carrying vegetables to sell in the city. Workers crowded the sidewalks on their way to their jobs. Suddenly a streetcar clanged around the corner. The frightened conductor leaned out.

"Go back! Go back!" he shouted to the crowd. "German trucks—a round-up!"

It was a Gestapo trick to descend on an area and arrest everyone in sight, in the hopes of picking up a few important members of the underground in the dragnet. Within seconds the street was deserted—except for one man. Pilecki kept on walking. This was what he had been waiting for. Germans appeared as though out of nowhere. A

German voice screamed, "Halt! Halt! You're under arrest!" Pilecki slowly raised his hands. The first phase of his plan had been accomplished.

Conditions at the camp were far worse than he had suspected. Outside, the temperature was below zero. The prisoners lived in unfinished barracks without stoves or windows. They had no winter clothes and often, no shoes. Their only food was watery soup and hard bread. At night they slept on straw, four or five men on a narrow plank, so tightly packed that they could not even turn over.

During the day, the weak and sick were forced to do hard physical work, building the half-finished camp. Many froze to death. Hundreds died of exhaustion, lung diseases, or starvation. The Nazis treated them like animals. Many prisoners had lost all hope of survival. No one seemed to care whether they lived or died—except, of course, Witold Pilecki.

There were two things about Auschwitz that made it different from other German prison camps. It was the first camp built mainly to house Poles. This meant that Pilecki found old friends and former soldiers there—men he could trust to help him. Second, it was the first camp built outside Germany. This meant that the people in the nearby villages were Polish, hostile to the Nazis and sympathetic to their imprisoned fellow citizens.

Pilecki's plan had five goals.

1. to organize the prisoners into a resistance group; if each prisoner knew there were trustworthy friends to turn to, he or she would feel less terrified and alone;

2. to cheer them up by bringing in news from outside about their families and friends, and about the progress of the war;

3. to get extra food and warm clothing;

4. to report to Home Army headquarters in Warsaw about conditions at Auschwitz;

5. to prepare units to defend the camp in case the Nazis should lose the war and attempt to destroy it.

The Nazis ran the camp with savage brutality. Prisoners were tortured and executed, often for no reason at all. The German guards used a disciplinary method called "collective responsi-

bility." If one person committed an offense, others in the camp were punished. It worked well. It weakened the will to resist and kept the prisoners from joining together to oppose their captors. Faced with such hopeless misery, many people would have given up, but not Pilecki. He had a job to do, but how and where would he begin?

He decided to use a "system of fives." He would pick five trustworthy men and reveal his mission to them. None of the five would know the other four, in case one of them was captured and tortured. Only Pilecki would know everything. He chose his men from the hospital, the work assignment office and the building office. The hospital was clean and warm, and a source of extra food and shelter. The Nazi guards shunned it because they were afraid of catching a contagious disease. The work office assigned prisoners to jobs in different parts of the camp. The building office was important because it gave Pilecki access to tools and equipment, and also because the people that worked there were the only ones who were allowed to work outside the camp. They could contact the local villagers. He chose men from each of these offices to complete his "fives." Many were old army friends.

By using his "system of fives," Pilecki was able to hide sick prisoners in the hospital and get medical care for them. Previously, when a man was too sick to work, the guards simply left him to die in the snow or shot him. Now Pilecki's men were able to save many of these sick prisoners' lives. Through the work office, Pilecki could get inside jobs for the older and weaker prisoners. A steady stream of news came and went through the building workers and the nearby villagers. Pilecki had accomplished the second phase of his plan.

During the next two years, many men joined Pilecki's groups of fives. There was always more work to be done. Thousands of new prisoners arrived every day. The men in the carpentry shop made little statues to sell the local citizens. Inside them they hid Pilecki's reports of the Nazi brutality in the camp. The figurines were taken secretly to the Home Army in Warsaw, and the reports were forwarded to London, where they were read over the radio to the free world. When the hospital was being rebuilt, the prisoners in the electrical shop stole parts and put together their own radio transmitter and receiver. They hid it beneath the floor of the ward where the infectious patients were kept. At night, they would sneak into the hospital and listen to the news from London. Through the transmitter, they sent reports to Warsaw. In this way, they were able to learn the truth about the progress of the war. It cheered the prisoners to learn that they were not the only ones fighting against the Nazis. The outside workers brought bread and vegetables, given to them by the nearby villagers, and shared them with the hungry inmates.

Pilecki was ready for the next phase of his plan. He had always believed that the Nazis would lose the war, and he was afraid that when the end came they would kill all the prisoners. He wanted to divide his resistance group into military units and train them to defend themselves against the guards. But before he could do this, a terrible thing happened. Toward the end of 1941, Adolf Hitler decided to turn Auschwitz into a death camp for Polish and German Jews. The building office work groups were ordered to build large gas chambers that contained rows of false shower heads. Jewish prisoners were given bars of soap and ordered to strip. They were told they were to take showers and be disinfected. Once they were inside, the Nazis bolted the doors. Instead of water, deadly gas sprayed out of the shower heads. The bodies were placed in large ovens called crematoria and burned to ashes. Thousands of men, women, and children died in the gas chambers. Their bodies were burned night and day. Auschwitz was no longer a dreadful prison camp. It had become a hell on earth.

This concentration of Nazi brutality on the Jewish prisoners made life easier for the non-Jewish Poles. They were no longer allowed to die in the snow or killed for no reason. With so many new prisoners arriving daily, the Germans needed all the workers they could get. Men and women were needed to work in munitions factories. Finally, even some Jews were spared, at least for a time. Only those who could not work were sent directly to the gas chambers. Pilecki's men did what they could to help the Jews, and shared extra

food, clothing, and medicine with them. Many Jews joined his fives.

At the beginning of 1943, Pilecki decided that he had to leave Auschwitz. His group was now very large. Too many people knew he had organized it. He himself knew too much, and he was not sure he could keep silent under Gestapo torture. Also, he believed that when the war ended the Nazis would murder all the prisoners. They would not want anyone alive who could talk about the horrors of Auschwitz. He wanted to report to his headquarters in Warsaw to get help.

On the night of April 26, 1943, Pilecki got himself assigned to a night work group in the camp bakery, with two close friends. Under their striped prison uniforms they wore suits made in the camp clothing shop. A prisoner who was a locksmith had made them a key to the bakery door. A prison doctor had given them a strong-smelling chemical that would kill their scent so the guard dogs would not be able to track them. Each man carried a poison pill. They did not intend to be captured alive.

At 2:00 A.M. they carefully opened the bakery door, only to find that a Nazi guard was standing there! It had begun to rain, and he had taken shelter in the doorway. The three men held their breath and prayed. After a few minutes the guard walked away. The prisoners rushed out into the rain. They were free at last!

They ran as far as the river along the outer perimeter of the camp. Then they threw their prison clothes into the cold black water. The sound of gunfire behind them told them they were missed. Their only hope was to cross the river, but the current was too strong to swim. Pilecki found a small boat secured to a ring in the bank with a chain and a strong lock. As the shouting Nazis drew nearer, Pilecki and the others struggled to free the boat. Suddenly Pilecki had a crazy idea. He shoved the homemade key that had opened the bakery door into the lock. By a miracle the key fit! The lock flew open. The chain fell off. The boat floated free. The Nazis would never catch them now!

Helped by friendly peasants, they made their

way to Warsaw, sleeping by day and traveling by night. Pilecki told about the Auschwitz atrocities and outlined his plan. The prisoners, he told his Commander, were too weak to fight alone. They needed Polish soldiers and weapons. The Commander shook his head sadly. There was no help to give. There were no extra men or guns for the prisoners. Whatever strength they had left after four years of devastating war must be used to free Poland from the Nazi occupation.

It was a terrible blow to Pilecki. He had done what he could. He had saved thousands of lives. He had given the prisoners the will to survive. He had chosen a good man to replace him. The prisoners were more likely to survive now than they had been before his arrival.

In November and December of 1944 the Germans destroyed the gas chambers, the crematoria, and all the camp records. Then they evacuated the camp, marching the prisoners southwest toward Germany. Some died along the way, and some survived. The First Ukrainian Front of the Russian Army pursued the retreating Nazis and overran Auschwitz.

Pilecki continued to fight the Germans and was captured while fighting in Warsaw. He was again sent to a prisoner-of-war camp but was freed at the end of the war. His reports and those of his "fives" on the brutality at Auschwitz helped to convict the Nazi leaders at the Nuremburg war crimes trials in 1946.

Pilecki continued to fight for a free Poland when his country came under the domination of the Russians in 1945. While he was on a secret mission, he was arrested by the Russian military police and imprisoned a third time. It is sad and ironic that this man who risked his life so many times to free his country was executed for treason in 1948. To this day, Poland remains under Soviet (Russian) influence. It is, to all intents and purposes, still an occupied land.

Chapter II

MADELEINE

It was the summer of 1943 in occupied Paris. A pretty young woman hid behind some leafy plants in the greenhouse of the Pasteur Institute. She had shoulder-length dark hair, olive skin, and large brown eyes.

A portable radio transmitter sat on the stone floor in front of her. She tapped urgently at the telegraph key, sending a coded message across the English Channel. A secret listener somewhere north of London would receive it. She was a British agent—a spy.

From time to time she looked anxiously toward the door. The Gestapo were searching for her. Their trucks were moving back and forth through the streets with their radio direction-finding antennas straining to pick up her signals and follow them to her hiding place. Quickly, she finished her message and signed off with her code name, MADELEINE. Then she took her transmitter apart and folded it into its carrying case.

MADELEINE was not her real name. She was

Noor Inayat Khan, and she was half Indian. In her own language this meant "Light of Womanhood." Her family had sent her to school in Paris. She made many friends there. Later she wrote children's books. French children loved her books so much that she was asked to read her stories aloud on the radio. But then the war came, and the Nazis invaded France. India was part of the British Empire, and that made Noor an enemy to the Germans. She escaped to England just before the first German troops arrived in Paris.

Safe in England, she could have resumed her career as a writer. But the country was at war. The Germans were her enemies too. She joined the Royal Air Force and was sent to radio school. Because she knew several languages, she was asked to volunteer for duty in British Intelligence. It was dangerous work, but Noor knew that she was needed. She knew she would make a better spy than most English girls. She could hide in Paris because she had many old school friends there.

After two months of training, she was

dropped behind the German lines in occupied France, to join the PROSPER network, which helped the French resistance to hold up the advance of the German armies. PROSPER blew up bridges and rail tracks, and sent important news about military movements to the British War Office.

Noor's message from the Pasteur Institute reported terrible news. Most of the agents of the PROSPER network and many of their French friends had been arrested by the Nazis.

A telephone on the wall of the greenhouse buzzed sharply. Noor put the receiver to her ear without speaking. It was her lookout, calling from an upstairs room in the Institute building, where he was watching the street below.

"Hurry! Get out! They've just turned the corner."

An ominous gray command car painted with the black swastikas of the German Army had entered the street. It crawled slowly toward the Institute. On its metal roof an antenna rotated slowly, round and round, tracking and searching.

Noor snapped the locks on the suitcase, which

held her transmitter. It looked like a small overnight bag. She slipped out of the greenhouse and across a grassy lawn, through a gap in a hedge into the next street. There she mingled with the afternoon crowds. No one would have suspected that she was a spy.

Noor ducked into an alley, past rows of rubbish bins, and into the back door of a small, red brick house. She ran up the stairs to an attic room. There a short, stocky, bearded man dressed in the blue smock of a French worker was waiting for her. He was her control, and his code name was SERGE. No one knew what his real name was.

"It was too close this time, MADELEINE," he said. "A few more minutes and you would have been in a Gestapo interrogation unit. The other PROSPER agents have all been arrested. Now the Nazis can use all of their tracking equipment to locate your transmissions. It is only a matter of days before they succeed in trapping you. You must leave. We can smuggle you to the coast of Normandy, and back to England."

England meant safety. A place where Noor would be able to sleep at night without the constant fear that the Gestapo would break down her door and drag her away to prison and torture. It was tempting. It was also impossible.

"I am the only trained radio operator left," she told the bearded man. "Somebody has to report to England. Without my transmitter, the Paris resistance would be cut off from English supplies."

"It could mean your life, and the lives of your friends."

"We are at war. There are thousands of soldiers whose lives are in danger. They can't ask to be sent home from the battle front just because they might get hurt."

SERGE looked at her sadly. "As you wish," he said.

He read the copy of the last message she had sent to England. Then he touched a match to it and watched it burn to ashes. Noor slipped out of the house and back into the crowded street.

In a country house somewhere north of

London, another woman in uniform of the First Aid Nursing Yeomanry, handed a folded yellow paper to her commanding officer.

"Latest message from MADELEINE, sir," she said, standing at attention.

"Are you sure she sent it? It could be the Germans sending us false information."

"I'm sure, sir. I was at radio school with her. I know her 'fist'—her touch on the telegraph key. That's why I was chosen to be her 'godmother' on this end, to receive her messages from France."

After dismissing the young woman, the colonel locked the door. Then he decoded and read MADELEINE's message. Opening a safe behind his desk, he drew out a green folder stamped MOST SECRET. A typewritten label on its cover said simply, MADELEINE. It gave Noor's history, her record in radio school, and how she had impressed the officer who approved her for intelligence duties with her courage and her quick mind. She had given up the chance for an officer's commission in the Royal Air Force when she chose to be a radio operator behind the German lines. The PROSPER network was her first assignment.

The colonel closed the folder and stared out of the window at the ancient elm trees in the garden. He thought of Noor. He remembered how she had been shunned at first by the other girls at the radio school. She was strange to them, a dark-skinned foreigner. Later, when they got to know her, they all loved her. Then he thought of the information he had received only that morning. The arrests of the other PROSPER agents were not just the result of good German police work. There was a traitor among them. They had been betrayed to the Gestapo!

MADELEINE was still free because she was a recent arrival in Paris. The traitor had given away the agents' names before she had come. But the Germans would find out about her soon. Perhaps they already had. There might still be time to bring her back to England and save her life.

But what about her messages? Could British Intelligence and the French resistance forces spare her before a new network could be set up? Even a week or a few days would be precious. Was her life important compared with the thousands of lives that might be saved by the informa-

tion about German troop movements she might send from Paris?

The colonel shook his head and put Noor's folder back in the safe. Noor would stay in Paris.

Noor moved around Paris, from hiding place to hiding place, helped by old school friends who knew they were risking their own lives by sheltering her. But she could not move fast enough. One afternoon, as she sat transmitting a coded message to England from a house in the Paris suburb of Clichy, the door of her room crashed open. She found herself face to face with a detachment of German soldiers. Behind them were two Gestapo agents in long, black leather coats. One of them pointed a Luger pistol at her. It was useless to resist. She was handcuffed and brought to Gestapo headquarters.

The Nazis questioned her about her work and about the people who had helped her. She refused to tell them anything. They beat her, but she still refused to talk. While she was being moved from the interrogation room to her cell, she broke away from her captors and tried to escape. She was recaptured and cruelly beaten again. Nothing the Nazis could do could force a single word from her.

One night Noor and two other British prisoners managed to climb out of a window to the roof of the building. They crawled to the edge of the roof. Then they jumped to the building next door. But the street below was full of German soldiers. They were captured. Once again Noor was severely punished.

The Gestapo commandant realized at last that she would never talk. He stamped her records PARTICULARLY DANGEROUS, and ordered her sent to a prison in the Black Forest region of Germany. There she was chained like an animal in a cell so tiny that she could neither stand up nor lie down. She had to stay in a crouching position. They kept her that way, half-starved, for ten months. Still she refused to talk.

At last the Germans lost patience with her. It was clear that they would not get any information out of her. They sent her to the death camp at Dachau, where she was executed by a firing squad.

When news of her death arrived in England, King George VI held a special ceremony at Buckingham Palace. He read the story of her courage aloud, and then, even though she was no longer alive, he awarded her a medal, the George Cross, which is given only "for the most conspicuous courage in circumstances of extreme danger."

Chapter III

PÈRE MARIE BENOIT and FERNANDE LEBOUCHER

In 1939 German troops invaded France. They took the northern, northeastern, and western parts of the country, including the Atlantic coast. But the remaining two-fifths of France was left unoccupied. The capital city of the unoccupied zone was Vichy. Its government cooperated with the Nazis and was recognized by them.

The real French government, led by General Charles de Gaulle, escaped to London. They called themselves the Free French. At home, in occupied France, the Vichy government was like a puppet and Hitler was the puppeteer who pulled its strings. Hitler believed that allowing the Vichy government to exist would make it harder for the Free French to threaten the German invaders at a later date.

Benito Mussolini, leader of the Italian fascists, was Hitler's ally. On June 10, 1940, the Italians went to war with the French too, and they demanded some of the occupied French territory. Hitler gave them a strip of land 50 miles (80 km) wide between Italy and France, in which the city of Nice was located. This strip was called the Italian sector.

As soon as the Nazis had settled into occupied France, they introduced anti-Jewish laws. French Jews had their rights as French citizens taken from them. They were forced to wear yellow, six-pointed stars sewn on their clothes. Their shops had to display signs in their windows that said, "This shop is owned by a Jew."

The Germans set up "collection camps" where Jews were held until they could be sent to Germany to work in munitions factories. Those who could not work were sent on to death camps like Auschwitz where they were gassed.

Thousands of Jews who were in danger of death or imprisonment fled to the unoccupied zone. Although the Vichy government was friendly to the Nazis, the anti-Jewish laws were less strictly enforced there. Also, the great port city of Marseilles was in the unoccupied zone. Ships came and went every day. It might be possible for Jews to find a boat bound for England or America.

If they could not, they might still escape to Switzerland or Spain or to Italy, where there were no death camps and gas chambers.

One day in late 1942, a young woman knocked at the door of the Capuchin monastery in Marseilles. The Capuchin friars were dedicated to Saint Francis of Assisi. They believed in peace, love and charity. Their mission was to live out the teachings of God. An old monk opened the door and looked anxiously at the woman's tear-stained face. She asked to see Père Marie Benoit, the head of the monastery. The old monk led her into a small sitting room, where Père Benoit soon joined her.

Père Benoit had been a professor of religion. He had studied in Rome, where he had learned Hebrew, so he could read the Old Testament, which was originally written in that language. He made many Jewish friends there. When he returned to France, he did everything he could to help the Jews who were being persecuted by Hitler. That was why the young woman had come to ask him for help. Her name was Fernande Leboucher.

Fernande's husband, Ludwik Nadelman, was missing. He was a Jew who had come to France from Poland when the Nazis invaded his country. They had met soon after his arrival and had married. They fled together to the unoccupied zone and made their way to Marseilles, where they hoped to find a ship leaving for America.

They had tickets and passports, but when they got to the ship there were hundreds of people ahead of them. The ship was anchored a few hundred feet from the shore, and they had to go out to it in a small fishing boat and then climb up to the deck on a long rope ladder. When their turn came, Fernande put her foot on the first rung of the ladder and froze. She was afraid of heights, the sea was rough, and the ladder swung precariously above her. She could not move. The people behind her called out to her to hurry, but it was no use.

Ludwik refused to go alone. Back in their apartment, Fernande begged him not to go out. The Vichy government was helping the Germans by rounding up Jews who were not French to work in German factories. Ludwik was a Pole.

Despite the danger, he left to find a Polish resistance group. Fernande had not heard of him since.

Père Benoit shook his head. "There is nothing we can do now, my child," he said to Fernande. "If he has been arrested and sent to a collection camp, he will be allowed to write to you in a few days. When you get his letter, come and see me. In the meantime, go home and pray."

Père Benoit was right. Ludwik had been taken to the camp at Rivesaltes, 160 miles (257 km) west of Marseilles. Through the camp chaplain, who was a friend of his, Père Benoit got Fernande permission to spend half an hour with Ludwik.

"We must find a way for you to escape," Fernande said. Ludwik shook his head. It was true that escape was possible, but the Germans had taken away his identity papers. Without them, he could go nowhere. He would only be arrested again.

Fernande returned to Père Benoit and told him what Ludwik had said. She asked him to help her find false papers for her husband.

Père Benoit agreed. What they must do, he told Fernande, was to make Ludwik appear to be a Christian. Capuchin parishes in France's unoccupied zone had baptismal certificates. Père Benoit could fill out a baptismal certificate with a false name and stamp it with the church seal. If Ludwik were stopped by the Gestapo, it would show that he was a French Christian and not a Jew.

But identity was not enough. Ludwik also needed a ration card issued by the police, bearing his photograph and his false name. Without it he could not buy food, clothing, or medicine.

Père Benoit had many important friends in Marseilles who were sympathetic to the Jews. He made several telephone calls. At last one of his friends called back. A ration card had been found! Père Benoit and Fernande carefully pasted Ludwik's photograph on it and wrote in the false name. Fernande left at once for Rivesaltes.

When she was alone in the visitors' room with Ludwik, she gave him the papers, but he refused to take them.

"How can I escape," he said, "when there are many good men here who need help? I will not be sent to Germany for several months, but there are others here who will go soon. We must help them first."

No matter how she pleaded, he would not go. Fernande returned to Père Benoit and told him what had happened. The old priest was not discouraged. Why not try to help everybody? Why not set up a large-scale plan to help many prisoners escape? Their families could bring them photographs of the men in the camp. Père Benoit could get baptismal certificates. They could paste the pictures on the ration cards. . . .

The ration cards. That was the problem. How could they get enough of them? There was only one way. They would have to contact the Resistance, the French underground army that was fighting the Nazis. The Resistance had members hidden in every major city and many villages in France. They were helped by British and American intelligence agents who brought them weapons and equipment. Père Benoit knew that there were Resistance members working in government offices in Marseilles, without the knowledge of the Vichy government. They were even in the Police Department. They could steal blank ration cards.

Their final problem was what to do with the escaped prisoners when they arrived in Marseilles. It would be impossible to hide them there indefinitely. Père Benoit went to Nice, which was in the Italian zone, to visit an old friend, Angelo Donati, a Jew and the head of the Franco-Italian Bank. He agreed to find shelter, clothing, and money for the men from the collection camp, and to help them escape over the border to Switzerland or Italy.

Fernande and Père Benoit put their plan into action. She went back and forth to Rivesaltes carrying forged ration cards and certificates. It was not hard to escape, because the camp was badly guarded. The guards were sure that the lack of identity cards would keep the prisoners from escaping, because they would not be able to get very far outside the walls without papers. The men climbed the walls or cut the barbed wire and made their way to Marseilles. Then Père Benoit

and Fernande gave them clothes and money enough to get to Nice. There, Angelo Donati helped them out of France.

So far, the escape plan had worked. But they were beginning to run out of money. Hundreds of new prisoners were arriving at the camp every day. Any Jew who was not a Frenchman was still in grave danger. Then Fernande had an idea. She had been well-known before the war as a dressmaker, and she had had many rich and fashionable customers. Why not open an expensive dress shop in Marseilles, with all the latest Paris fashions? It was something she knew about and could do well.

"We could make a lot of money, Father," she said, "and it would be a good way to cover our operations. Who would believe that a fancy dressmaker would be helping men escape from Rivesaltes?"

She hired an assistant named Victoire, and together they worked in Fernande's tiny apartment making dresses and hats. When they were ready, they gave a fashion show at the Grand Hotel in Marseilles. The richest and most important people were invited. It was a great success. Fernande sold almost all her dresses and hats and was commissioned to design many more. The wives of high officials of the Vichy government came to order clothes from her. She gave all the profits to Père Benoit.

"Father," she said, "we're back in business."

Then a terrible thing happened. One of the escaping prisoners was captured by the Gestapo. They tortured him, and he broke down and betrayed Père Marie Benoit! From that moment, the Gestapo never stopped watching the monastery and the old priest. At any hour of the day or night they would suddenly break in and search the place. It was a miracle that they did not find the illegal papers hidden there.

Now the escapees could no longer come to the monastery. Fernande had to meet secretly with members of the Resistance and pass the papers to the refugees through them. Also, Ludwik had found out that he was to be sent to Germany soon. He escaped and hid at the house of a member of the Resistance. It was too dangerous for Fernande to stay with him, but she went to see

him early in the morning. To her horror, he had been found out by a police informer, who was suspicious of his Polish accent.

Ludwik was sent to Germany. In despair, Fernande tried to kill herself. But soon she recovered her will to live—and to help others. After the suicide attempt, she went back to work.

With the guards alerted, there were no more escapees from the camp. But there were many refugees from the occupied zone. The suspicious Gestapo watched the old priest and the dressmaker like hawks. Even so, with the help of the Resistance, they got hundreds of Jews safely out of France.

In November 1942, Hitler ordered his armies to invade the unoccupied zone of France. The British and Americans were preparing for an attack. From then on, no Jew was safe in France. The Gestapo arrested, tortured, and killed any Jew they could find. Word came through Resistance agents that the names of Fernande Leboucher and Père Marie Benoit were on the Gestapo wanted list. They had to go into hiding. They knew too much. If they were tortured into telling what they knew, many Resistance members would lose their lives. Père Benoit did not know what to do, but the Capuchin Order decided for him. They transferred him to Rome.

Fernande and Père Benoit loaded their papers into two trucks and drove to an old estate outside of Marseilles—not a moment too soon. Hours after they left, the Gestapo arrived at the convent. Père Benoit had barely escaped.

While he waited for permission to cross into Italy, Père Benoit hid in the trucks with Fernande, and together they continued their work. Several weeks later, he left for Rome. Fernande stayed in France but did not return to Marseilles. She hid from the Germans until the end of the war.

Fernande Leboucher was a true heroine of the Resistance. With the help of Père Benoit, she had saved thousands of lives. By using her great skill as a dressmaker, she had earned so much money that she was the major source of funds for the whole escape project.

Fernande never saw Ludwik again. He was executed in a death camp in Germany. Père Benoit continued his resistance work in Rome. After the war, he was decorated by the French, Israeli, and Italian governments.

Chapter IV

PAUL MASON

While Hitler and his Nazis were marching across Europe, the Japanese were trying to conquer the Far East. They had gained a foothold in China with their invasion of Manchuria in 1931. In 1937, they attacked again. This time they took the Yangtze River Valley and Wuhan.

The Japanese needed the oil and rubber of the East Indies to support their war effort. The first phase of their plan was to capture the islands of the South Pacific. They moved into French Indochina in July 1940. The United States responded by stopping the sale of petroleum to Japan. It now appeared that war was inevitable. So the Japanese decided to launch a surprise attack.

On December 7, 1941, Japanese bombers attacked the American air and naval base at Pearl Harbor. Eighteen ships were sunk and 174 planes destroyed. There were 3,581 casualties. The next day, the United States declared war on Japan. The fight for the Pacific had begun.

Before the Americans could build new ships

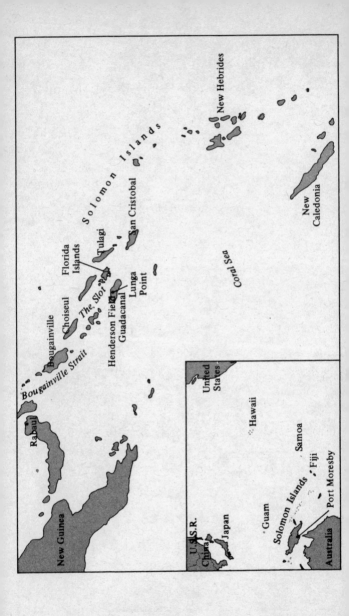

nd planes, the Japanese swept halfway across
1e Pacific. Within two months, they had occupied
iuam and Wake Island, Hong Kong, Manila,
orneo, New Ireland, New Britain, and Singa-
ore. They set up a major air and naval base at
.abaul on New Britain. To protect this base
nd to isolate Australia, they needed to capture
1e chain of islands off Australia's northeastern
oast: New Caledonia, the New Hebrides, the
ijis, and the Solomons.

If you look at the map you will see that the
olomon Islands stretch like a necklace from
ougainville, east of Rabaul, to San Cristobal,
00 miles (965 km) southeast. Below Bougain-
lle the islands split into two parallel lines. There
a narrow strip of water called "the Slot" in
etween.

In 1942, the Solomon Islands were controlled
y the British and Australian forces. Their head-
uarters was at Tulagi, one of the Florida Is-
nds near Guadalcanal.

Look at the map again and find Tulagi.
hen find Port Moresby, New Guinea. The Jap-
nese plan was to seize Port Moresby and invade

Tulagi. From Port Moresby they could easil
bomb Australia. From Tulagi they could attac
and conquer the Fiji Islands and Samoa, cuttin
the vital supply route between Australia and th
United States. Without supplies, it would be im
possible for the Allies to mount a counteroffen
sive from Australia.

It was a good plan, and it might hav
worked, if it had not been for our next group c
resistance heroes, the Coastwatchers of the Solo
mon Islands.

The Coastwatchers were civilians—planter
and missionaries who lived and worked on th
South Pacific islands. They had been organized b
the Australian Navy to watch the unguarded Aus
tralian coast in case enemy ships or planes shoul
try to invade it. By mid-1941, there were 800 o
them at 100 stations.

They set up watch posts at the highest point
of their islands and radioed information abou
Japanese naval movements. Received by contro
stations on the larger islands, the information wa
forwarded to the main Coastwatcher station a
Townsville in Australia. As the fighting pro

gressed, the Coastwatchers became the most important secret weapon the British and American forces had.

The man in charge of all Coastwatchers was Lieutenant Commander Eric Feldt. When the Japanese began their drive for Pacific conquest, Feldt warned his Coastwatchers that to continue their work would expose them to great danger. They were civilians. They could leave the islands for the safety of Britain or Australia. Some left, but most of them decided to stay on and resist the Japanese.

By 1942, Feldt's Coastwatchers were ready for war. He gave his force a code name. He called it FERDINAND, after the bull in the children's story who preferred smelling flowers to fighting. "Be like Ferdinand," he told his Coastwatchers. "Do not fight the Japanese, watch them. Watch them and report everything they do. As Coastwatchers, your fiercest weapons are your eyes."

Feldt set up new stations, on Bougainville, in the central Solomons, and on Guadalcanal. On April 30, 1942, following their battle plan, the Japanese sailed for the Solomons. On May 4, they occupied Tulagi. But they were driven out of New

Guinea (and Port Moresby) by the American Navy in a great battle called the Battle of the Coral Sea.

How many ships do the Japanese have? How many men? Where are they? What are they doing? What is happening on Tulagi? The Americans were planning an attack, but without the answers to these questions they could not proceed. No one could help them more than the Coastwatchers.

In order for the Guadalcanal Coastwatcher stations to answer the questions about Tulagi, they had to get very close to the Japanese. To do this would mean risking capture. But the local natives came and went freely inside the Japanese bases. The Coastwatchers hired the natives to help them. The Solomon Islanders were Melanesians, a primitive, dark-skinned people who lived by fishing and planting vegetable gardens. They knew every inch of the forbidding jungle areas and the high, rugged mountains. They already knew and trusted the Coastwatchers, many of whom had lived in the islands long enough to speak the native language. They agreed to help.

The Guadalcanal natives worked as scouts. They paddled across the Slot at night, crept through the jungle, and spied on the Japanese. Then they described everything they saw to the Coastwatchers in great detail.

Suddenly, in June, the Japanese landed troops on Guadalcanal, at a place called Lunga Point. The Coastwatchers there were now in enemy territory. They moved higher and deeper into the interior. The natives came to report that the invaders were building an airfield. This information was radioed to Commander Feldt. The American Navy had planned to recapture Tulagi, but now the plan had to be changed. They had to seize the airfield first. If it had not been for the Coastwatchers, the Americans on the way to Tulagi might have been surprised by Japanese planes and defeated. Instead, the marines drove the Japanese out of Lunga Point.

One of the Bougainville Coastwatchers was a man named Paul Mason. He had set up his station on a hill. From there he could see all Japanese ships and planes on their way from their

main base at Rabaul to Guadalcanal. Mason was a small, mild man. He had worked in the Solomon Islands for most of his life as a plantation manager. On the morning of August 7, four hours after the Americans landed on Guadalcanal, he suddenly saw Japanese planes. Immediately, he flipped on his radio, and sent his message: "27 BOMBERS HEADED SOUTHWEST." Within twenty-five minutes the Americans were ready for battle. The marines at Lunga Point stopped unloading their ships. Anti-aircraft guns were readied. Grumman Wildcat fighters took off from their carriers. Two hours later it was all over. Sixteen Japanese planes were shot down and the others driven off. A victory for the Americans, thanks to Paul Mason.

Again and again Mason sent his messages. The Japanese suffered heavy losses. By the end of August, the marines had completed the airfield at Lunga Point on Guadalcanal. They named it Henderson Field, after a marine who had been killed in the battle for Midway Island. The Americans now had control of the air. Unfortunately, the Japanese controlled the sea. They wanted to attack and neutralize or recapture Henderson Field, but the warnings of the Coastwatchers prevented them from doing so.

One morning a group of natives rushed up the hill to Mason's station. "Better clear out!" they told him. "The enemy has come! They are bringing their beds ashore!"

It was true. The Japanese had landed on Bougainville. And they had with them the heavy equipment needed to build an airstrip! Mason was not surprised. Bombers based on Bougainville would be 500 miles (805 km) closer than Rabaul to Guadalcanal.

"Mason, sir!" It was a breathless native. "Sir! A Japanese patrol is coming. They say they are coming to find the Coastwatcher."

Mason lost no time. He packed his radio and plunged into the jungle, his native scouts leading the way. He put on a brave smile for the natives, but he knew his days of peaceful watching were over. His life would be a deadly game of hide and seek. Would the natives be loyal or would they sell him to the Japanese for a reward? There was no time to worry. He set up a new station in a mountainous area near the coast.

From his new station he could see the Shortland Islands, where a great many Japanese ships were anchored. He could also see across the Bougainville Strait to Choiseul. The Japanese were hiring native labor for the new airfield on Bougainville, and Mason sent some of his native friends to work for them and bring him reports, which he quickly radioed to Commander Feldt.

AERODROME IS EXPECTED TO BE COMPLETED WITHIN A WEEK. STORES AND FUEL SPREAD ALONG FORESHORE BETWEEN UGUMO RIVER AND MOLIKO RIVER. ENEMY TROOPS NUMBER ABOUT 440.

Mason could see that the Japanese were anchoring more ships at their harbor in the Shortland Islands. With Mason's information, American planes were able to destroy many of these ships and to slow down work on the airstrip.

Although the marines had occupied Henderson Field at Lunga Point, the Japanese troops they had driven back were still on Guadalcanal. Now the Japanese Navy was trying to supply those troops, sending ships in at night when they could not be seen and counted by the Coastwatchers.

By the end of October, there were still 23,000 Japanese on Guadalcanal, compared to only 11,000 U.S. marines! America controlled the air, but Japan still ruled the sea.

On Bougainville the Japanese were making an all-out effort to find Paul Mason, using specially trained dogs to track him. As luck would have it, a bomb dropped in an American raid hit the kennel and killed all the dogs. Still, the patrols got closer and closer. Mason had to move out again, further into the jungle. At last the Japanese decided that he had left the island, and gave up. Within minutes of their departure, he was back on the radio again.

In November Mason reported a major Japanese force on the way to attack Henderson Field. The marines, with the help of newly landed reinforcements, dug in. For three days and nights they fought in what was to be known as the Naval Battle of Guadalcanal. It was a bloody battle, but the Americans won. The Japanese failed to retake Henderson Field and were driven out of Guadalcanal.

Meanwhile, Mason was in trouble on Bougainville. The natives were tired of waiting for the Americans to come. The Japanese fed them and gave them gifts. Except for a few loyal scouts, they went over to the Japanese side. Once again Mason had to pull out and move further into the jungle. Just before Christmas he received a message from the Japanese commander. "Come and have Christmas dinner with us and bring your friends," it said. "If you don't, we'll shoot you on sight." Mason just laughed. He made his way to the northern part of the island, where he joined forces with Jack Read, another Coastwatcher.

It was no use. Repeated Japanese patrols and the now unfriendly natives kept Mason and Read constantly on the move. Most of their equipment was discovered and destroyed. They could not radio information to Commander Feldt because the Japanese had imported new tracking equipment with which to follow their signals. With another Coastwatcher, named George Stevenson, Mason decided to cross the towering mountain range that stretched across the southern half of

Bougainville. Then he would continue south, away from the enemy. He divided his party into two groups, leading the first one himself. Crossing the range at 6,000 feet (1,847 m), he set up camp and sent a guide back to lead Stevenson's group to the camp, only to discover that the second party had been ambushed and their leader killed.

Breaking radio silence, Mason reported the tragedy. The reply he received saddened him. He was ordered to join the other Coastwatchers at Kereaka near the coast. There he would wait for a submarine to pick them up. Mason felt he had lost his battle. After a year and a half of hard work, the Japanese were driving him out.

With the rest of his scouts, Mason crossed half the length of Bougainville. They made their way through deep gorges, over paths lost in vines and creepers, through swamps and across cold mountain ridges. Several times he met Japanese patrols and had to retreat. He lost men and equipment, including his precious radio.

Finally, on July 19, the exhausted party reached Kereaka.

On July 24, the American submarine *Guardfish* picked up the weary Coastwatchers. The men were brought to safety. Mason always felt that he had failed in his mission. But to the flyers of Henderson Field he was a hero. His warnings enabled the Americans to capture and hold Guadalcanal in spite of four Japanese attacks. His messages had slowed down Japanese shipping, forcing the enemy to turn their attention to the Central Solomons. His information on the Bougainville airstrip and the naval build-up in the Shortland Islands kept the enemy from getting a firm foothold in the Solomons. As one American admiral said, "The Coastwatchers saved Guadalcanal, and Guadalcanal saved the Pacific."

In October, General Douglas MacArthur awarded Mason the Distinguished Service Cross, the second highest decoration given by the United States. However, Mason's real reward came when the Japanese were driven out of the Solomon Islands. That was what he had risked his life so many times for—to see Bougainville once again peaceful and free.

Chapter V

GEOFFREY KUPER

Watching Japanese troop movements was not the only job assigned to the Coastwatchers. Some of them rescued American pilots shot down by the enemy. This was an especially dangerous task.

The man who saved more flyers than any other Coastwatcher was Geoffrey Kuper, whose station was at Tataba on Santa Isabel Island in the Solomons.

Kuper was the only Coastwatcher born in the Solomon Islands. He was half native. His father was a German planter who had married a local native woman. Geoffrey was born in 1917.

Unfortunately, a person who was half native was treated very badly by the white planters, even if he were highly intelligent and the son of a white man. The only way that Geoffrey could get a good education or learn a trade was for him to become a "native medical practitioner" or, as the local people called them, an NMP. The NMP's were medical assistants who helped the British district medical officers, but they were not real doctors.

Geoffrey Kuper was the NMP on Rennell Island south of Guadalcanal when war began in the Pacific. He served under Donald Kennedy, the district officer for the Western Solomon Islands. One day Kennedy sent for Kuper to offer him a new kind of job. Many European planters had fled before the Japanese advance, leaving behind them native workers who had come from other islands. These natives were now stranded. They had no food or money. Kennedy was supposed to move them back to their own islands, where they could find their home villages. Kennedy chose Kuper as his assistant in this project. Kennedy was also given a radio and made a Coastwatcher. Kuper agreed to work with him, spying on the Japanese.

In the course of relocating the native workers, Kuper landed on the island of Ranongga. There he met a young woman, the daughter of a local family. Her name was Linda Martin, and she too was part native. They fell in love. Soon after, a missionary came to Ranongga and married them.

The Kupers and Kennedy did not know that the Japanese had begun their advance down the

Solomons to attack Tulagi. On their way back to Santa Isabel, their boat was attacked and strafed by a Japanese Zero fighter, but no one was hurt.

When the Japanese captured Tulagi, the Kupers and Kennedy were in deadly danger. Their base at Mahaga was deep in enemy territory. Worse still, the NMP on nearby Savo Island had joined the Japanese. He betrayed the Santa Isabel Coastwatchers by telling the Japanese about the hiding places that Kennedy and Kuper would probably choose for themselves and their equipment.

On May 17, six weeks after the Kuper wedding, the Japanese landed a force of 100 men just below Mahaga. They were led by the traitorous Savo Island NMP. Kennedy, Kuper and Linda, and a few of their loyal helpers got ready to defend themselves. They had only five rifles. They prepared to destroy their radio and their fuel and food supplies so that they would not fall into the hands of the enemy. However, the Japanese soldiers were called back to Tulagi before they could find the Coastwatchers. On their way they found the *Waiai,* the boat that Kennedy and Kuper had used to relocate the natives. They set the boat on fire and sank her.

Fortunately, Kennedy had another boat, a small ketch called the *Marara*. He loaded everyone aboard. Since Mahaga was no longer safe, they sailed northwest up the coast. For the next month they were always on the move, shifting their activities from place to place, radioing their reports of Japanese ship movements. In the middle of June, Kennedy decided that Kuper was well-trained enough to man a Coastwatcher station of his own. He gave him a radio and sent him with Linda and a three-man crew to the island of New Georgia.

On August 7, the Americans recaptured Tulagi and landed in Guadalcanal. Kuper was back on Santa Isabel repairing his boat. He saw a raging air battle between American Grumman Wildcats and Japanese Zeros. As he and his native crew stared at the sky, three planes burst into flames and fell into the water. He searched for survivors, but was unable to find any. Two days later a native came running up to him.

"Kuper, sir!" he said. "We found a white man on the beach. He fell out of the sky in one of the great air machines. What shall we do with him?"

"Is he American or Japanese?" Kuper asked.

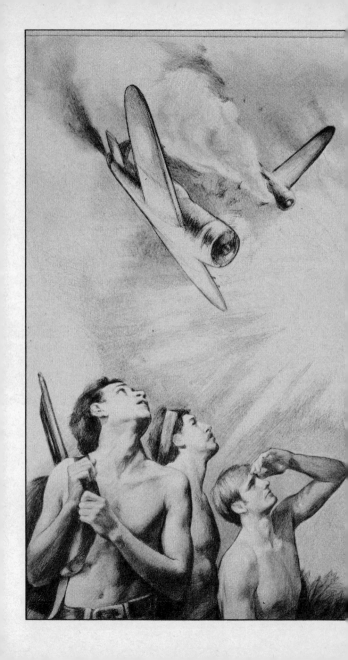

The native thought for a moment. "I do not know," he said, shaking his head. Like many natives he couldn't tell the difference between an American and a Japanese.

"Wait here," Kuper said. He went to his cabin and wrote a note. It said:

To the Flyer Shot Down:
Whether you be American or Japanese,
report to me immediately.

Geoffrey Kuper
Base Defense Officer
Santa Isabel

In a few hours the native was back with an answer.

I am unable to travel.

Gordon E. Firebaugh
Lt. (J.G.) USN

Kuper followed the native to the wounded man. He was a fighter pilot from the carrier *Enterprise*, who had been shot down on August 7. His legs were badly burned, but he had managed to swim ashore. Kuper and Linda doctored his wounds and fed him. Then they radioed headquarters in Tulagi to send an aircraft to take him back to his ship. They did not know that a major naval battle was raging between the Americans and the Japanese. There were no planes available. Kuper was told to bring Lt. Firebaugh to Tulagi in his small boat, the *Joan*.

It was a difficult and dangerous trip. At low tide, Kuper had to wade ahead of the *Joan*, pulling at the anchor chain while his little crew pushed with poles. At dawn, they hid the boat and disappeared into the jungle until it was dark again. At one point in the journey, Kuper told the others to wait, and he went into the jungle alone. In a little while he returned in a canoe paddled by a smiling Chinese gentleman. He was Chan Cheong, a storekeeper who had fled from Tulagi with his family when the Japanese came. He was glad to help Americans in any way he could. In this case, his help was a rooster. It was a tough old bird, but it tasted good to Kuper and his friends, who had been living on yams during their journey.

They made it to Tulagi. When a U.S. Marine inspection party boarded the *Joan*, Kuper greeted them in a freshly pressed uniform, saluting proudly. He looked calm and serene. No one would have guessed he had spent forty-eight sleepless hours struggling through enemy territory.

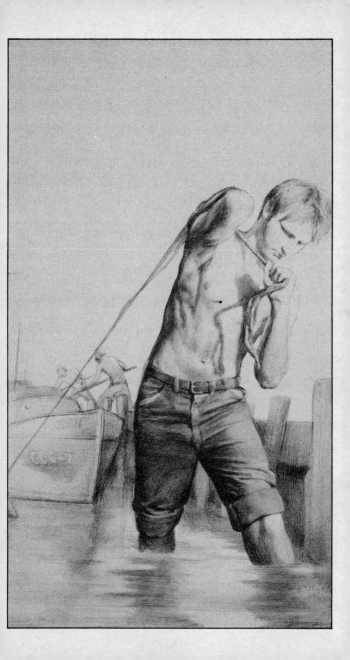

On August 18, Kuper was formally made a Coastwatcher and directed to set up a station at Tataba on Santa Isabel. He sent out native scouts daily to search the shoreline for downed pilots or to spot Japanese ships or planes. He began his operations at the time when air and sea battles were being fought for control of Henderson Field on Guadalcanal. Most of the fighting took place over or near Santa Isabel. When pilots were shot down, the natives would bring them either to Kuper or to Chan Cheong's house. Kuper, using his medical training, would doctor their wounds and radio for planes to pick them up. When planes were not available, Kuper and Linda would keep the wounded men as guests and nurse them until they could be sent back to their ships or to Henderson Field.

One day a marine pilot's plane ran out of fuel and splashed down near the shore. Kuper and the scouts dragged the plane ashore, happy to have rescued it to fly again. Immediately, he radioed Henderson Field that a badly needed fighter plane was waiting to be picked up. Although the pilot was rescued, no one ever came for the plane.

hirty-four years later it was still on the beach.

And so it went. Kuper's scouts would find owned flyers, Linda would welcome them and ok for them, and Kuper would radio to have em picked up. In November, the weary Japa- se slacked off their attempts to take Henderson eld, and for a while Kuper had no downed pi- ts to care for. But the Japanese had built a sea- ane base at Rekata Bay on the northeast coast Santa Isabel. Kuper decided to scout the base. e sent a native to bring gifts of fish and fruit the Japanese commander, who gave the native e run of his base. Of course the native reported erything he saw to Kuper, who promptly ra- oed it to his superiors. As a result, the American mbers repeatedly raided the base. This slowed wn Japanese movements in the Central Sol- ons.

Soon the fighting picked up again. Kuper d his wife resumed their rescue operations. hen there were no planes available, Kuper sent s charges back to Tulagi in native canoes. His twork worked smoothly because the Santa Isabel tives were loyal to him. This had not happened

in Bougainville where the natives had gone over to the Japanese, but Kuper himself was part native. They thought of him as one of their own.

He understood their ways. The natives were primitive. They did not understand that Coastwatchers were supposed to watch, not fight. Kuper let them ambush Japanese patrols and kill the enemy soldiers. This made them feel that they were winning the war. They looked on Kuper as their general.

Although Kuper's family background helped him with the natives, it was still a mark against him with the Australians in Townsville. They never treated him as an equal. Of the fourteen Coastwatchers in the Solomon Islands, he was the only one who was not given a commission in the Australian Navy. Commissions were for white people only, not for half-castes.

Geoffrey Kuper was a true hero of the resistance. He and his crew saved the lives of twenty-eight American pilots in only a few months and, in doing this work, boosted the morale of the Henderson Field flyers. Although the battles were fierce and bloody, the men always knew that if they were shot down, Kuper and his scouts would bring them home.

Bibliography

Garlinski, Jozef. *Fighting Auschwitz.* New York: Fawcett, 1975.

Leboucher, Fernande. *Incredible Mission.* New York: Doubleday, 1969.

Lord, Walter. *Lonely Vigil.* New York: Viking, 1977.

Stevenson, William. *A Man Called Intrepid.* New York: Ballantine, 1976.

Index